Lewis M. McCornick

Descriptive List of the Fishes of Lorain County, Ohio

Lewis M. McCornick

Descriptive List of the Fishes of Lorain County, Ohio

ISBN/EAN: 9783741124297

Manufactured in Europe, USA, Canada, Australia, Japa

Cover: Foto ©Andreas Hilbeck / pixelio.de

Manufactured and distributed by brebook publishing software
(www.brebook.com)

Lewis M. McCornick

Descriptive List of the Fishes of Lorain County, Ohio

LABORATORY BULLETIN No. 2.

OBERLIN COLLEGE.

DESCRIPTIVE LIST OF THE FISHES

OF

LORAIN COUNTY, OHIO.

BY LEWIS M. McCORMICK,

ASSISTANT IN THE MUSEUM.

OBERLIN, OHIO.
PUBLISHED BY THE COLLEGE.
1892.

ADVERTISEMENT.

The present Bulletin is the second of a series, which, it is hoped, may be issued from time to time, giving the results of special work in the laboratories and museum of Oberlin College. The first of the Series was a "Preliminary List of the Flowering and Fern plants of Lorain County," issued in 1889, which, however, did not bear the title of "Bulletin No. 1" at the time of its publication. That number, however, will be assigned to it henceforth.

The present paper is the result of Mr. McCormick's pains taking collection and study of our native fishes, extended through several years, as opportunity has allowed, and resting upon specimens preserved in the museum. It is published in harmony with the conviction, here cherished, that one of the most important duties of any museum is to secure a full representation of the natural objects occuring in its own vicinity, and to make them available to the cause of science.

ALBERT A. WRIGHT,

May, 1892.   Professor of Geology and Natural History.

INTRODUCTION.

It is the object of this paper, first, to present a reasonably complete list of the fishes which occur in Lorain County, Ohio, with such notes on habits, distribution, etc., as may be helpful to future investigators, or in some degree additional to those in Jordan's very complete report on the fishes of Ohio. (Geological Survey of Ohio, vol. IV.)

Second, to give such characteristics of the families and species noted as will enable even the uninitiated to recognize the fishes that he may catch, by the "ear marks." In doing this I have taken the diagnoses given in Jordan's paper mentioned above, as models, making such changes as the more restricted scope of my work allows. It should be borne in mind that these characterizations (printed in italics) are from a limited fauna, and that points good for this locality may be found in fishes which do not occur here, though an effort has been made to avoid this as much as possible. While it is hoped that this feature will simplify somewhat the difficulties in the way of making the acquaintance of our aquatic neighbors, it is not intended to replace the keys of more systematic works. Every student of natural history should have a Jordan's Manual of the Vertebrates * at least.

Jordan's report in the Ohio Geol. Survey contains an account of the literature of Ohio fishes up to 1878, with very full synonymy of the species, and many notes on habits, to which the student is referred for much material not within the scope of this paper. To facilitate such reference, the species numbers in Jordan's Manual and in his Report on the Ohio Fishes are given with each species.

In his report, Jordan gives 165 species that are supposed to inhabit the waters of Ohio. Of these 96 are given as being found in Lake Erie and its tributaries, 123 in the Ohio river drainage, about 40 characteristic of the lake region, 56 common to both regions, and 67 found only in the river drainage. Of these lists Dr. Henshall says: "In an enumeration of this list recently sent

*A Manual of the Vertebrates of the Northern United States, by D. S. Jordan; 576 pages, A. C. McClurg & Co., Chicago. $2.50,

to me by Dr. Jordan, after eliminating doubtful and extra-limital species, it is reduced to 130 species. But he named some 15 other species as likely to occur in Ohio waters."

Since 1882 the most impotant additions to the literature of the subject are (1), Notes in "Fisheries and Fishing Industries of the United States," by Prof. G. B. Goode and associates; (2) three papers by Dr. J. A. Henshall, published in the journal of the Cincinnati Society of Natural History, the first being a list of 90 species taken near Cincinnati in 1888; the second an additional list of 40 Ohio fishes, including 22 from Lake Erie, 1889; the third, Observations on Ohio Fishes, 1890, in which the history of the subject is reviewed. In 1890 a partial list of Lorain County fishes appeared in the same journal giving 55 species, without notes.

The nomenclature of American ichthyology is in a very unsettled state, almost every paper that appears having some changes for old friends. In order, therefore, to facilite references to Jordan's Manual, I use the names given there, although I realize that this will mark the paper as not "up with the procession."

The present paper includes 88 species; and is, I believe, the first distinctly local list published for Northern Ohio. The same list, with notes on distribution only, has been sent to the U. S. Fish Commission for publication 'n their reports. There are, perhaps, a dozen more species whose known geographical range makes it probable that they occur in this region, but for lack of definite records they are omited here.

This list is based on notes covering about four years of observation, but in no one season have I been able to give the subject the attention that would have enabled me to note the movements of the fishes to and from their spawning ground. I only know that many species do enter the streams from the lake for this purpose, and then go back to deep water. Under what conditions they make these pilgrimages, what length of time is spent in the streams, how they protect their eggs, etc., etc., are questions still to be solved.

In speaking of the comparative abundance or rarity of species, I can only give my own experience; and such an instance as the trout-perch, for example, which I did not find at all the first three years, but did find commonly in the same waters the last year, makes me feel like making few arbitrary statements on this point. Specimens of all the fishes named in this list except *Polyodon spathula* and *Salvelinus namaycush,* are preserved in the Oberlin College Museum.

Lorain County is wholly within the lake watershed, all its streams flowing northward into Lake Erie. The streams are all small, the largest being Black River, navigable for about three miles, and Vermillion River, having only about a mile of safe water. But these are important as harbors for the lake trading vessels and fishing boats. The land is quite flat, with a gentle slope toward the lake, and the streams are mostly shallow and sluggish, the exceptions being found in the parts that cross the "ridges" or old lake beaches, and a few of the small streams that are tributary to the Vermillion. Some of these are quite brisk and have worn for themselves deep channels in the shale.

, Spring Brook is one of these, and deserves special mention. It is the little stream that rises (see map) near the center of Henrietta township and flows northwest: it is spring-fed and does not run dry, though so small that it can be stepped across at almost any part of its course. The first half mile meanders through a meadow, and in this part there is a colony of red-bellied and red-sided minnows, species not detected elsewhere in the county. A few suckers. seven other kinds of minnows, a few green-sided sunfish, Johnny darters, and a few star-gazers are the only other fish noticed. Catfish, pickerel. gars, etc., seem to be excluded by a series of small water falls in the lower part of the stream. That the minnows are not hindered by these falls I surmise from the observation of excitement exhibited by a lot of red-bellied and red-sided minnows placed under a hydrant in a pail. As soon as the water began to splash they acted as if they had springs in them, leaping out of the pail a foot or more.

The streams may be divided into "head waters," the slower portions back from the lake; "the riffles," where the streams are more broken by cutting through the shale beds, and the "lower parts," comparatively deep and still, where the depth of water is influenced by the direction of the wind on the lake. Each of these is characterized by certain kinds of fish, though some species are found in all waters. Mill-dams in both of the rivers also form well defined limits for certain species.

Lake Erie where it touches Lorain County is shallow, reaching a depth of about 55 feet 3 miles from shore, and is free from islands. Not even a rock breaks the surface two rods from low-water mark on the whole coast. The beaches are sandy, but a rod or two out there is usually a line of stones that make seining difficult. Pound nets are set in "strings" from, perhaps, ½ mile from shore to 3 miles, and it is from these that I have obtained most of my lake fishes.

It is only necessary to mention one other kind of water, the ponds and bayous left by changes in the courses of the larger streams, where water plants flourish, and some species, such as the mud-minnows and pickerel, find congenial surroundings.

Camden lake yields "pumpkin seeds" (*Lepomis gibbosus*), and shiners, (*Notemigonus chrysoleucus*), though "bull-heads" and "pike" are said to occur also.

Many of the species make desirable aquarium stock, and are more beautiful and interesting than the common gold fish. Among these are young catfish, especially the channel cats, the red-bellied minnows, the young sunfish, perch and the darters.

In gathering these notes I have had material assistance from Mr. W. H. Warden, of Lorain, who has not only extended every courtesy to me when I have visited his fish wharves, but has kindly saved many valuable specimens from his pounds. Prof. S. E. Meek examined and verified my *Cyprinidæ*, and the officers of the U. S. Fish Commission have assisted by the loan of a seine, and in other ways. Col. McDonald has kindly given permission to copy the plates used in this paper from the publications of the U. S. Fish Commission.

These acknowledgements would be incomplete without a reference to the constant encouragement and advice of Prof. A. A. Wright, which has made the completion of the work possible.

ABBREVIATIONS.

Jord. Man. — Jordan's Manual of the Vertebrates of the Northern United States. Fifth edition, 1888.

O. St. Surv. — Report on the Fishes of Ohio in Vol. IV. of the Geological Survey of Ohio.

In the plates, the line below each figure represents an inch in length, on the scale to which the fish is drawn.

SYSTEMATIC ARRANGEMENT

OF THE FISHES DESCRIBED IN THE FOLLOWING PAGES.

—

CLASS **CYCLOSTOMI.** THE MYZONTS.

ORDER **HYPEROARTIA.** MYZONTS.

FAMILY **1. Petromyzontidæ.** THE LAMPREYS.

CLASS **PISCES.** THE TRUE FISHES.

SUB-CLASS **TELEOSTOMI.** THE PERFECT-MOUTHED FISHES.

SERIES **Ganoidei.** THE GANOID FISHES.

ORDER **SELACHOSTOMI.** THE SHARK-MOUTHED FISHES.

FAMILY **2. Polyodontidæ.** THE PADDLE-FISHES.

ORDER **GLANIOSTOMI.** THE STURGEONS.

FAMILY **3. Acipenseridæ.** THE STURGEONS.

ORDER **GINGLYMODI.** THE GARS.

FAMILY **4. Lepidosteidæ.** THE GARPIKES.

ORDER **HALECOMORPHI.** THE BOWFINS.

FAMILY **5. Amiidæ.** THE BOWFINS.

SERIES **Teleostei.** THE BONY FISHES.

ORDER **NEMATOGNATHI.** THE THREAD-MOUTHED FISHES.

FAMILY **6. Siluridæ.** THE CATFISHES.

ORDER **EVENTOGNATHI.**

FAMILY **7. Catostomidæ.** THE SUCKERS.

FAMILY **8. Cyprinidæ.** THE MINNOWS.

ORDER **ISOSPONDYLI.**

FAMILY **9. Hiodontidæ.** THE MOONEYES.

FAMILY **10. Clupeidæ.** THE HERRINGS.

FAMILY **11. Salmonidae.** THE SALMONS.

FAMILY **12. Percopsidae.** THE TROUT-PERCHES.

FAMILY **13. Cyprinodontidae.** THE KILLI-
FISHES.

FAMILY **14. Umbridae.** THE MUD MINNOWS.

FAMILY **15. Esocidae.** THE PIKES.

ORDER **APODES.** THE EELS.

FAMILY **16. Anguillidae.** THE TRUE EELS.

ORDER **HEMIBRANCHII.** THE HALF - GILLED
FISHES.

FAMILY **17. Gasterosteidae.** THE STICKLE-
BACKS.

ORDER **PERCESOCES.** THE PIKE-PERCHES.

FAMILY **18. Atherinidae.** THE SILVERSIDES.

ORDER **ACANTHOPTERI.** THE SPINY-RAYED
FISHES.

FAMILY **19. Centrarchidae.** THE SUNFISHES.

FAMILY **20. Percidae.** THE PERCHES.

FAMILY **21. Serranidae.** THE SEA-BASS.

FAMILY **22. Sciaenidae.** THE DRUMFISHES.

FAMILY **23. Cottidae.** THE SCULPINS.

FAMILY **24. Gadidae.** THE CODFISHES.

DESCRIPTIONS OF THE SPECIES.

Family I. PETROMYZONTIDÆ. The Lampreys.

Systematic zoologists do not include lampreys with the fishes, but put them into a separate Class, differing from the true fishes in having very imperfectly developed skeletons. The skeleton in this Class is simply a cartilaginous vertebral column, without distinct skull, jaws, shoulder girdles, limbs or ribs. The gills have the form of fixed sacks, with circular openings, six or more on each side of the "neck."

1. Petromyzon concolor (Kirtland). Lamprey.
[Jord. Man. 5. O. St. Surv. 2.]

Eel-shaped, bluish silvery or mottled with yellowish, mouth disk-shaped, set with about four circles of small teeth. *Two teeth close together in front of the opening of the gullet.* Reaches the length of 14 inches.

This species comes into the rivers from the lake in the latter part of May, when they may be found attached to old logs and stones ; at other seasons they are seldom seen, but are occasionally found attached to large fish in pound nets.

On the 22nd of May, 1887, I took several that were full of ripe eggs, (about the size of No. 8 shot,) in Vermillion river.

Family II. POLYODONTIDÆ. The Paddle-fishes.

2. Polyodon spathula (Walbaum). Paddle-fish.
[Jord. Man. 39. O. St. Surv. 3.]

A queer fish, with a long paddle-like snout overhanging a broad mouth ; *head with flap and snout more than half the total length ;* body spindle-shaped, mostly smooth, olivaceous.

I know of but one ever caught in the Great Lake region. That one was taken in a pound net near Vermillion, in 1874, and was stuffed as a curiosity and exhibited in a store window for some years ; it is still in existence.

FAMILY III. ACIPENSERIDÆ. THE STURGEONS.

3. Acipenser rubicundus Le Sueur. LAKE STURGEON.
[Jord. Man. 42. O. St. Surv 4.]

Sturgeons are large spindle-shaped fish, with big, sucker-like mouths, without scales, but having rows of shields on the back and sides; not easily mistaken for anything else. (See plate 5.)

We have but one species, which is very common. The young have much sharper and comparatively larger spines than the older ones. The largest specimen I have seen measured 6 ft. 2 in., and weighed 129 lbs. Formerly sturgeon were but little valued, but now there is a ready market for all caught at $1.50 each, the pedlars taking them into the country. Almost every pound-boat that comes in has a few sturgeon, the most being caught in May. One man, near Dover, uses a gill net with a seven-inch mesh for taking them.

FAMILY IV. LEPIDOSTEIDÆ. GARS.

4. Lepidosteus osseus (Linnæus). GARPIKE. BILL-FISH.
[Jord. Man. 44. O. St. Surv. 7.]

A long, slim fish, with the body covered with diamond-shaped bony scales; color leaden in old specimens, marked with black spots which are more distinct in the young. The head is long and slender, the *snout from eye to tip more than twice the length of the rest of the head.*

Gars are common in the lake and lower parts of the larger streams. Large schools come into the rivers in April to spawn. They grow to be from 2 to 5 feet long.

5. Lepidosteus platystomus Rafinesque. SHORT-NOSED GAR.
[Jord. Man. 45. O. St. Surv. 8.]

Very much like the preceding species, from which it may be told by the shorter snout, only about equal to the rest of the head. (See plate 1.)

Very rare.

FAMILY V. AMIIDÆ. THE BOWFINS.

6. Amia calva Linnæus. DOGFISH.
[Jord. Man. 47. O. St. Surv. 10.]

Rather elongated, dark lead-colored above, nearly white below. Sides with greenish wavy markings, most conspicuous in the young; males have a round black spot on the tail. Mouth large, set with strong teeth. Head covered with bony plates, *a broad, bony plate between the arches of the lower jaw.* Length 1 to 2½ feet. (See plate 2.)

Rare; once in a great while one is brought in from the pounds, and I have taken one in a seine in Black River.

FAMILY VI. SILURIDÆ. THE CATFISHES.

Everybody knows a catfish—the smooth skin, big head, strong spines and fringe of (8) barbels about the wide mouth, marking a very conspicuous group. Some of the species grow very large and are highly prized as food. Catfish are taken in pound nets and on set lines, and with pole and line tackle. Leeches and salamanders form favorite bait for set lines, though fresh meat is used also. The smaller species of *Ameiurus* are called Bullheads indiscriminately.

7. Ictalurus punctatus (Rafinesque). CHANNEL OR SILVER CAT.
[Jord. Man. 51. O. St. Surv. 14.]

Slender and graceful, *tail forked. A continuous bony ridge from back of head to dorsal fin.* Silvery white or olivaceous, with small, dark, round spots; old specimens darker. Reaches a weight of about 5 pounds.

Common, being one of the species taken on handlines. The young are plentiful in the streams below the dams, but have not been detected above.

8. Ameiurus nigricans (Le Sueur). BLUE CAT.
[Jord. Man. 52 O. St. Surv. 15.]

Slaty bluish, young lighter, body stouter than in the channel cat and the *tail not so deeply forked; bony ridge from skull to dorsal spine broken.*

Common in the lake and lower parts of the rivers. This species attains a weight of 100 pounds or more, but I have never seen a specimen of more than 40 pounds from the lake, and 5 pounds is probably a fair average. Highly prized as food.

9. **Ameiurus natalis** (Le Sueur). YELLOW CATFISH.
[Jord. Man. 54. O. St. Surv. 16.]

Body rather chubby, yellowish brown, sometimes almost black, *tail rounded, anal rays 24 to 27.* Length 15 inches.

Common in the ponds, streams and lake.

10. **Ameiurus vulgaris** (Thompson). LONG-JAWED CATFISH.
[Jord. Man. 55. O. St. Surv. 17.]

Body moderately elongated ; color blackish, paler beneath; *lower jaw longest; anal rays* 20.

Martin's Run: only one recorded.

11. **Ameiurus nebulosus** (Le Sueur). COMMON BULL-HEAD.
[Jord. Man. 56. O. St. Surv. 18.]

Dark brownish yellow, varying to blackish, tail not forked, *lower jaw not projecting, anal rays* 21-22, *pectoral spines short, about half as long as head.* Length 18 inches.

Common in all streams.

12. **Ameiurus melas** (Rafinesque). SMALL BLACK BULL-HEAD.
[Jord. Man. 57. O. St. Surv. 19.]

Very much like the preceeding species in general appearance. The pectoral spine is shorter, 2½ to 3 in head, and the anal fin is noticeably shorter—of 17 to 19 rays. Length 12 inches. (See plate 6.)

Common in all streams and ponds.

13. **Leptops olivaris** (Rafinesque). MUD-CAT.
[Jord. Man. 59. O. St. Surv. 22.]

Very long and slender, *the head flat and wide, lower jaw projecting,* color brownish, mottled with yellow, lighter beneath ; anal fin of 15 rays ; length, 2 to 3 feet.

Quite rare. I have seen but one specimen fresh, though I have noticed heads on the beach. The fishermen say that they sometimes catch very large mud-cats.

The Stone-cats, *Noturus*, are distinguished from the other genera by the second dorsal fin, which is connected to the back along its whole length, often joining the tail.

There are three species in our waters. All have venom pores in the pectoral spines, a stab from which stings like a wasp. In the aquarium they are always most active at night.

14. **Noturus flavus** (Rafinesque). YELLOW STONE-CAT, HAMMER-HEAD.

[Jord. Man. 60. O. St. Surv. 23.]

Body elongated, head flattened, nearly as broad as long. *Band of teeth on front of upper jaw*, U *shaped*. Color yellowish brown. Length 12 inches.

The most common stone-cat: found in the larger streams and in the lake. They are sometimes taken in the pounds and are often killed and thrown onto the beach by the waves during storms.

15. **Noturus minurus** Jordan. VARIEGATED STONE-CAT.

[Jord. Man. 63. O. St. Surv. 25.]

Body slender, grayish *body with four black cross bands, black on top of head, tip of dorsal and middle of caudal*; length 5 inches.

Quite rare. I have taken a few in both Vermillion and Black Rivers. On July 4th, 1891, I picked up a dozen full-grown ones that were floating in the water near the mouth of Black River, evidently stunned by the waves that a storm was dashing against the piers. A puncture from the pectoral spine of one 1¼ inches long reminded me of the sensation of a hornet's sting for two hours. They are one of our prettiest aquarium fishes.

16. **Noturus gyrinus** (Mitchill). CHUBBY STONE-CAT.

[Jord. Man. 65. O. St. Surv. 26.]

Head large, broad and deep; color brownish yellow, *with a narrow, black lateral streak; pectoral spine smooth*; length 5 inches.

Common on the mud banks in the lower parts of streams entering the lake.

FAMILY VII. **CATOSTOMIDÆ.** THE SUCKERS.

Suckers are oblong or elongated fish, usually with lips thickened into a "sucker mouth;" scales smooth in most species, large and coarse; ventral fins abdominal, belly not sharp, head scaleless, the single dorsal fin with more than 11 rays. (See plate 3.)

17. **Carpiodes thompsoni** Agassiz.   LAKE CARP.
[Jord. Man. 71.   O. St. Surv. 32.]

Oblong with high arched back *and long dorsal fin*, (*27 rays*). Dull white-colored with large coarse scales.   Length 15 inches.

Not very common, though a few are taken every season in the pounds.

18. **Catostomus teres** (Mitchill).   COMMON SUCKER.
[Jord. Man. 76.   O. St. Surv. 39.]

Body elongated, scales crowded in front, *65-70 scales in lateral line*, whitish, young dusky, often blotched with darker : length 1 to 1½ feet.

Very common in all our waters.

19. **Catostomus nigricans** Le Sueur.   STONE-ROLLER.
[Jord. Man. 77.   O. St. Surv. 40.]

Body stout in front, tapering off rapidly behind ; *head very large, body marked with three broad black bands*, scales moderate, crowded in front ; length one to two feet.

This fish is not uncommon in the channels of the larger streams. I have not found it in the smaller streams, nor below the rapids ; it seems to delight in swift running water, and is sometimes speared among the other suckers on the riffles.

20. **Erimyzon sucetta** (Lacépède).   CHUB SUCKER.
[Jord. Man. 78.   O. St. Surv. 41.]

Body rather compressed, oblong, head short, *color plain dusky or brassy, not lustrous ; no lateral lines*.   The young have a broad lateral band of black.   Reaches 10 inches in length.

Not common.   I have taken a few in the lower part of Beaver Creek.

21. **Minytrema melanops** Rafinesque.   STRIPED SUCKER.
[Jord. Man. 79.   O. St. Surv. 42.]

Body little compressed, about four times as long as deep, lateral line wanting in the young, nearly completed in the adult, color dusky above, sides and belly silvery, *a black spot on each scale along the sides, making longitudinal stripes*.   Length about 15 inches.

Rare.   I have taken two adults, one in Vermillion River, the other in Beaver Creek, and a few small ones in the latter stream.

22. **Moxostoma anisurum** (Rafinesque). WHITE-NOSED SUCKER.

[Jord. Man. 80. O. St. Surv. 44.]

Body heavy and compressed, somewhat arched. *Dorsal fin of more than 15 rays (15-18); upper lobe of caudal fin longer than lower;* color dusky bronze. Length 20 inches.

Not as common as the next two.

23. **Moxostoma macrolepidotum** var. **duquesnei** (Le Sueur). BIG-MOUTHED MULLET. "BLACK HORSE."

[Jord. Man. 81. O. St. Surv. 46.]

Body somewhat compressed. *Head large (4 to 4 3-4 times in length). Mouth large with thick lips.* Olivaceous, fins orange red. Length of largest measured, 2 feet. (See plate 3.)

Very common in the lake and larger streams.

24. **Moxostoma aureolum** (Le Sueur). SMALL-MOUTHED MULLET. LAKE RED-HORSE.

[Jord. Man. 82. O. St. Surv. 45.]

Like the preceding, *but the head is shorter and smaller. Mouth small. Head 4 1-2 to 5 1-4 times in body. Dorsal fin usually with 13 rays.* Length 2 feet.

NOTE.—It is difficult to distinguish the three *Moxostomæ* at sight, careful examination and measurements often being necessary to make discriminations certain. These are the "Suckers" or "Mullets" that crowd up the larger streams in such numbers in April to spawn on the riffles; by the middle of May most of them have returned to the lake, but small ones, up to 8 inches or more, can be found all summer. Dr. Kirtland, speaking of *aureolum,* says: "At the first approach of spring it resorts to the mouths of rivers and smaller streams in great numbers to spawn. We have seen them congregating in large numbers on riffles in the Cuyahoga River, near the eight-mile lock, even before the ice had left the stream."

I have not been able to watch the large streams closely in the early spring, but I do not think that suckers get on to the riffles now in any number before the water gets the "chill taken off." My experience has been that the same kind of weather that brings the snipe on to the marsh, draws the fish on to the riffles. The fish seem to spawn at night, and often may be seen lying in clusters of five or six, obliquely across the current, in the most rapid part of the stream.

A lot of 50, taken April 13th in Vermillion River, averaged two pounds apiece, and contained 14 *macrolepidotnm*, 36 *aureolum;* of the 50 the lateral line of one contained 45 scales; of one, 46; of twelve, 42, and the rest 43; otherwise essentially as described in the manual.

When first taken in a seine, young *Moxostoma* are usually plain silvery, but if kept for a while in an aquarium they will show dark colored bands very similar to those on *Catostomus nigricans.*

25. **Placopharynx carinatus** Cope. BIG-JAWED SUCKER.
    [Jord. Man. 85. O. St. Surv. 48.]

Measurements for this species are the same as for *Moxostoma macrolepidotum*, but the body seems more compressed and the outlines have different curves, so that the fish, once recognized, can be told from other mullets at sight. In those examined the outline of the lower lip is straighter than in other mullets, but the fish can only be surely identified by examining the lower pharyngeal bones which are large and broad, *with* (8-14) *thick, roundish teeth*, instead of many thin, flat ones. Length 2 feet.

Lake Erie. Common among other mullets.

FAMILY VIII. CYPRINIDÆ THE MINNOWS.

Minnows have scaleless heads, rather thin lips, are never sucker-mouthed. *Not more than ten rays in the single dorsal fin; anal fin short*, scales on the body smooth, and mouth toothless. Most of the species are small, but two or three grow to be quite sizable, one at least sometimes attaining a length of a foot. (See plate 3.)

Among the Minnows are some of our most beautiful fishes. In the spring, especially, some of the species are gorgeous in reds, yellows, and silver, and ornamental tubercles often give the little fellows a truly fantastic appearance.

From an economical point of view they are chiefly valuable as furnishing green pasturage for larger species. Minnows form our largest family of fishes, and in some casses it is very difficult to discriminate between the species: "in the young it may be impossible" (Jordan).

Intestines more than four times the length of body.

26. **Campostoma anomalum** (Rafinesque). STEEL-BACKED MINNOW.
    [Jord. Man. 87. O. St. Surv. 50.]

A rather dark colored little fish, with squarish looking scales, body somewhat compressed, *the long intestine wrapped around the air bladder;* adults 4–8 inches long.

Common in most of our streams.

Intestines more than twice the length of body.

27. **Chrosomus erythrogaster** Rafinesque.   RED-BELLIED MINNOW.

[Jord. Man. 89. O. St. Surv. 51.]

Clear brownish olive with dark mottlings above; below this, silvery *with two black lateral stripes on the sides.* This silvery color takes a charge of bright scarlet on the males in the spring. *Scales minute.* length about 3 inches. In a well lighted aquarium these fish will show their scarlet colors the year around; in the winter they flush or grow pale very quickly when excited by light, food, or fright.

Of this fish Kirtland writes (1850): "During the months of April and May every stream in northern Ohio swarms with this species—they crowd up the riffles in immense numbers to spawn. At that season the colors are very brilliant, but by midsummer they fade so much that the carmine tints are lost and the black stripes become a muddy brown. About the 1st of July, this species, in common with almost the whole Minnow tribe, forsake the rivers and descend into the lake."

I have found them in but one stream, Spring Brook. where they stay the year round. (See introduction.)

28. **Pimephales promelas** Rafinesque.   BLACKHEAD.

[Jord. Man. 93. O. St. Surv. 53.]

Body short and deep, *head short and blunt, lateral line incomplete, intestines long* (more than twice the length of body). Olivaceous, adults dusky with black heads: about 2½ inches long.

· Not common, but found in most of the streams.

29. **Pimephales notatus** (Rafinesque).   BLUNT-NOSED MINNOW.

[Jord. Man. 94. O. St. Surv. 60.]

Body compressed, elongated, head long, *scales before dorsal fin crowded, about 23; intestines long,* color dusty yellow, sides bluish, *a black spot on front of dorsal and base of caudal fin.* Length 4 inches.

Very abundant in all small streams.

Intestines short, less than twice the length of body.
Scales not closely overlapping nor deeper than long.
Teeth 4-4.

30. **Notropis deliciosus** (Girard). DELICATE MINNOW.
[Jord. Man. 103. O. St. Surv. 63.]

Body little compressed, head somewhat elongated, eye larger, color pale, with a silvery strip through which runs a *dusky line of light V-shaped* spots, length 2½ inches, scales 4. 34, 3.

"An insignificant little fish." Very abundant in all the streams.

31. **Notropis stramineus** Cope.
[Jord. Man. 103, O. St. Surv. 64.]

This species can be distinguished from the preceding only by careful comparison. There are more scales in the lateral line (5. 36, 4), and the fins are shorter.

Not common.

Teeth 1, 4, 4, 1.

32. **Notropis hudsonius** (De Witt Clinton). "SMELT."
[Jord. Man. 108.]

Body elongated, compressed ; head short with blunt snout. Pale yellowish green, silvery, young with *large round black spot at base of tail*, fins plain and small, length 10 inches.

Common in the lake and at the mouths of the rivers.

Scales overlapping, and deeper than long.

33. **Notropis whipplei** (Girard). SILVERFIN.
[Jord. Man. 110. O. St. Surv. 67.]

Body nearly elliptical, mouth small, the lower jaw the shorter, color bluish silvery, finely dotted with black on the edges of the scales, *a dark blotch on the upper part of last rays of dorsal fin*, wanting in young specimens. Length 3 inches.

Found in all the streams examined, but not very common.

Teeth 2, 4, 4, 2.

34. **Notropis megalops** (Rafinesque). SHINER.
[Jord. Man. 113. O. St. Surv. 75.]

Body compressed, comparatively short in adults, long in young, head large, color bluish silvery with darker shades, adult *scales much higher than long, anal fin has 9 rays*. Length 8 inches.

Very common everywhere. Males in Spring have rosy color on fins and belly. Shiners often take the flies cast for bass.

35. **Notropis ardens** (Cope). REDFIN.
[Jord. Man. 123. O. St. Surv. 74.]

Body elongated and compressed, fins large, *anal fin with 11 or 12 rays, a distinct black spot at base of first rays of dorsal,* scales small, 30 before dorsal fin, lateral line decurved ; females pale, males steel blue, belly and lower fins fine brick-red in the Spring. Length 2½ inches.

Not very common ; found in Black River and in Vermillion River near Kipton.

Scales larger and loosely set. "The species of this group are extremely closely related, and in some cases scarcely distinguishable.—Jordan.;

36. **Notropis dilectus** (Girard). ROSY-FACED MINNOW.
[Jord. Man. 128. O. St. Surv. 69.]

Slender and graceful, of a translucent olive-green with broad silvery bands on the sides ; *head larger than in related species ;* dorsal fin inserted behind ventrals ; length 3 inches. My specimens show 19 to 20 rows of scales before dorsal, instead of the " about 15 " of the manual.

Common in the lake and lower parts of all streams entering it. Found accompanying the next species.

37. **Notropis atherinoides** (Rafinesque). EMERALD MINNOW.
[Jord. Man. 129. O. St. Surv. 70.]

Very much like the preceding but with shorter, blunter head and of much larger size, reaching a length of 6 inches ; very abundant at times, so that the schools darken the water. The fishermen say that their coming into the rivers is a "sure sign" of a storm.

38. **Notropis arge** (Cope). SILVERY MINNOW.
[Jord. Man. 130. O. St. Surv. 70.]

Like the preceding species, but with a comparatively larger head, much larger eye and slender form ; length 3 inches.

Found in company with *atherinoides*, but not nearly so common.

39. **Ericymba buccata** (Cope). SILVER-JAWED MINNOW.
[Jord. Man. 132. O. St. Surv. 70.]

Body spindle-shaped, rather long, head long with broad muzzle. *Bones of the jaws with 7 or 8 mucus chambers appearing as silvery bars in four rows across lower half of the head.* Length 5 inches.

Taken once in Black River, near Elyria.

Barbel at angle of premaxillary present.

40. **Rhinichthys atronasus** (Mitchill).   BLACK-NOSED DACE.

[Jord. Man. 137.   O. St. Surv. 79.]

Body thick, moderately elongated, head large, eyes small. *Premaxillaries not protractile, a minute barbel on the angle, snout short, scales small,* (63 *in lateral line*): color dark, blackish above, mottled on the sides, with a band of orange and black on the sides; sometimes whole body bright crimson.   Length 3 inches.

I have found this species only in Spring Brook and Chance Creek.   Not common.

41. **Hybopsis amblops** (Rafinesque).   BIG-EYED CHUB.

[Jord. Man. 142.   O. St. Surv. 81.]

Slender, with big head flattened above, *eye longer than snout, premaxillaries protractile, sides with a dusky lateral band overlaid by silvery;* color pale straw.   Length 4 inches.

Common in some of the streams.

42. **Hybopsis storerianus** (Kirtland).   LAKE-MINNOW.

[Jord. Man. 143.   O. St. Surv. 62.]

Body rather elongated, head short, broad between the eyes, eye equal to snout, *pale, sides bright silvery, no darker band.* Length 8 inches.

One small specimen taken in Beaver Creek.   A few are sometimes taken in the pound nets.   On July 8, 1891, after a storm, a great many large ones were thrown on the beach by the waves, along with stone-cats and trout-perch.

43. **Hybopsis kentuckiensis** (Rafinesque).   HORNY HEAD.

[Jord. Man. 144.   O. St. Surv. 82.]

Body thick, head large and broad, snout long and blunt, *barbel conspicuous, color bluish dusky with coppery tints, not silvery;* males in Spring with large tubercles on head.   Length 10 inches.

Very common in the larger streams.

44. **Semotilus atromaculatus** (Mitchill).   CHUB.

[Jord. Man. 149.   O. St. Surv. 84.]

A heavily built, chunky fish, head large, scales small, crowded before the dorsal, *a distinct black spot at base of dorsal, anal with 8 rays;* dusky brown.   Length 12 inches.   (See plate 3.)

Abundant in most of the streams.

45. **Phoxinus elongatus** (Kirtland). RED-SIDED SHINER.

[Jord. Man. 150. O. St. Surv. 85.]

Body long and compressed, head long and pointed, "*much larger than in any other of our Cyprinidæ*," scales *very small* (*63-70 in lateral line*), lateral line decurved ; bluish, mottled with lighter, a broad lateral band, the front half of which is bright crimson in the Spring. Length 4 inches.

Common in Spring Brook, but not found elsewhere. (See introduction.)

46. **Notemigonus chrysoleucus** (Mitchill). GOLDEN SHINER.

[Jord. Man. 159. O. St. Surv. 87.]

Body much compressed, head short, low and flat, mouth small, *lateral line much decurved, scales on belly behind ventrals meeting in a sharp keel*, greenish with golden reflection. Length 10 inches.

Very common in all still waters.

47. **Cyprinus carpio** Linnæus. GERMAN CARP.

A large, coarse looking fish, with heavy scales, sometimes with only a few large scales, and a long dorsal fin ; not easily mistaken for anything else.

Occasionally taken in the rivers, where they are making themselves at home since their escape from several artificial ponds in 1887, during "the flood." I have seen them speared among the suckers on the riffles, and a few large ones are taken each year in the pounds.

FAMILY IX. **HIODONTIDÆ.** MOONEYES.

48. **Hiodon tergisus** Le Sueur. MOONEYE.

[Jord. Man. 161. O. St. Surv. 90.]

Body oblong, compressed, head short, *eye much longer than snout, color brilliant silver, teeth well developed, 12 rays in dorsal fin*, anal fin long. Length 15 inches. (See plate 4.)

Common in the lake, ascending streams sometimes.

FAMILY X. **CLUPEIDÆ.** THE HERRINGS.

49. **Dorosoma cepedianum** (Le Sueur). GIZZARD-SHAD.

[Jord. Man. 175. O. St. Surv. 88.]

Body oval, deep, compressed, *mouth toothless, belly serrated, dorsal fin with long thread-like last ray*, anal fin long and low. Length 15 inches. (See plate 1.)

Quite common in the lake, ascending the rivers. Kirtland says that it appeared in Lake Erie in 1848, coming through the newly-opened canal, and speaks of great numbers being killed by the cold in the canal as a proof that they belonged in a warmer climate. It is a very handsome but very worthless species.

FAMILY XI. SALMONIDÆ. THE SALMONS.

Fishes with abdominal ventral fins, two dorsal fins, the anterior rayed, the other adipose, scales cycloid (with smooth edges), and stomachs with many pyloric cæca, belong to this family.

"In beauty, gameness, activity and size of individuals, different members of this group stand easily with the first among fishes." And by virtue of its wide distribution and abundance the family as a whole rank among the first in economic importance.

50. Coregonus clupeiformis (Mitchill). WHITEFISH.
[Jord. Man. 183. O. St. Surv. 93.]

Body oblong, compressed, more or less elevated according to age, head small and short, *lower jaw shortest, tongue toothless, the gill rakers long and slender*, length 20 30 inches. Five or six pounds is the weight of a good-sized fish, though occasionally one much larger is taken. Mr. Nicholas of Vermillion reports one that weighed 19½ pounds. Jordan in three different works gives the lateral line as "74." In the specimens that I have examined I have found only one that agreed with this, one had 77, but those with 81 up to 85 were more common.

Common in the lake, not detected in the streams.

51. Coregonus artedi Le Sueur. LAKE-HERRING.
[Jord. Man. 186. O. St. Surv. 96.]

Slender, compressed, little elevated, greenish, sides silvery, finely speckled with darker, *lower jaw projecting.* Length 18 inches. (See plate 7.)

Very abundant in the lake, sometimes filling the pound nets almost solid with fish. I have not detected it in the streams.

52. Salvelinus namaycush (Walbaum). LAKE-TROUT.
[Jord. Man. 191. O. St. Surv. 101.]

Body long and thick, head long. *mouth well armed with teeth, gray, sometimes almost black, everywhere covered with rounded paler spots*, scales very small. Length 3 feet or more.

Very rare. I have but two records, and it is almost unknown to the fishermen here, though common in the eastern part of the lake.

FAMILY XII. PERCOPSIDÆ. THE TROUT-PERCHES.

53. Percopsis guttatus Agassiz. TROUT-PERCH.
[Jord. Man. 195. O. St. Surv. 103.]

Head conical, naked, *scales rough, an adipose fin present,* silvery, upper parts marked with dark spots made up of minute dots; length of largest taken 4 inches, but Jordan gives 10 inches as the length.

Common in Lake Erie, Black River, and Beaver Creek this year (1891-2). I did not detect it before, and do not think it was "common." Specimens taken in the latter part of April show well-developed spawn.

FAMILY XIII. CYPRINODONTIDÆ. THE KILLI-FISHES.

54. Fundulus diaphanus (Le Sueur). BARRED KILLI-FISH.
[Jord. Man. 203. O. St. Surv. 104.]

Rather slender, depressed in front, compressed behind, rather light colored, with 8 to 16 (25 in eastern forms) narrow, dark cross-bands *on sides, dorsal fin soft and set far back.* Length 3 inches.

Taken once near Lorain. I found this little fish common near Huron and Put-in-Bay in the soft-bottomed, grassy inlets. One was seined out of open water in Put-in-Bay. All specimens taken here show broader, darker markings than eastern forms, several having only 8 bars on the sides.

FAMILY XIV. UMBRIDÆ. THE MUD-MINNOWS.

55. Umbra limi (Kirtland). MUD-MINNOW.
[Jord. Man. 212. O. St. Surv. 107.]

A handsome, thick-set fish, dark greenish olive with mottled sides, *a distinct black bar at base of tail,* fins all soft, dorsal set far back. Length 5 inches.

Very common in the soft black mud in sloughs and bayous, also very hard to get hold of in said mud. Early in the spring they may sometimes be found in large numbers in the channels that run through the snipe marshes, and are even found in the open streams.

FAMILY XV. ESOCIDÆ. THE PIKES.

Long, rather slender, somewhat compressed fishes with long heads and wide mouths well filled with teeth, dorsal fin single, soft and set far back, lateral line more or less imperfect.   (See plate 8.)

56. Esox vermiculatus Le Sueur. LITTLE PICKEREL.
[Jord. Man. 214. O. St. Surv. 108.]

Olive green ; sides with many darker curved streaks and spots; *cheeks and opercles entirely scaly.*   Length 12 inches.

Common: found in the head waters of most streams and among the pads of spatter-docks in the bayous.   Not often taken in open water, or in the larger streams.   In June very small ones may be caught, but later all seined in a given stream will be very evenly matched, due I think to cannibalistic tendencies.   One, 6½ inches long, was seined in the act of digesting the head of another that was 4½ inches long : the rest of the body was waiting its turn outside.   Where common, as in the east branch of Vermillion River, near Kipton, none but the hardiest species hold their own against them.

57. Esox lucius Linnæus. COMMON PIKE. PICKEREL.
[Jord. Man. 216. O. St. Surv. 109.]

Greenish grey, mottled and streaked with yellowish spots and bars.   *Opercles without scales on lower half, cheeks scaled.*   Length 30 to 50 inches.

Pickerel are often killed in the ponds and channels of the snipe ground when, for a few days, about the first of April, they are spawning.   They are speared, shot or clubbed, the nature of the water making it impossible to use tackle.   But their season is short, and during the rest of the year "lucius" is quite safe, being seldom taken. I have seen two brought in from the pounds, one taken on a troll in the lake, and have seined two in the lower part of Black River.

58. Esox masquinongy (Mitchill). MASKALONGE.
[Jord. Man. 217. O. St. Surv. 110.]

Dark greyish black above, *sides light with dark round spots,* belly white, *cheeks and opercles scaleless on lower half.*   (See plate 8.)

Kirtland, writing of the Maskalonge, in 1851, says: "Forty years since, this fish was far more abundant than at present." And now the old fishermen of Lorain say that they "used to be much more common than they are now;" that they used to get some every time they lifted the pounds, while now half a dozen is the highest number taken in a season. Some years none at all are caught. Five were taken during the month of April, 1892, that weighed about 5 pounds apiece. In April, 1891, one was brought in that weighed 78 pounds and was about 6 feet long.

FAMILY XVI. ANGUILLIDÆ. THE EELS.

59. Anguilla rostrata (Le Sueur). COMMON EEL.
[Jord. Man. 218. O. St. Surv. 11.]

Body linear, covered with small imbedded scales, placed obliquely, at right angles to each other, giving a mottled appearance to the body; dark above, light below. Length 40 inches. (See plate 2.)

Large eels are occasionally taken in the pounds. I have never seen young ones, and do not think that they breed in the lake region.

FAMILY XVII. GASTEROSTEIDÆ. THE STICKLEBACKS.

60. Eucalia inconstans (Kirtland.) BROOK STICKLE-BACK.
[Jord. Man. 239. O. St. Surv. 164.]

A vary dark-colored little fish with a remarkably slender caudal peduncle and a fan-shaped caudal fin, *four distinct low spines before the dorsal fin.* Length 2½ inches.

. I have found stickle-backs in but two places; the bayou near Turkey Ridge farm, in Pittsfield township, (see map, just across the stream from "W" of the word West), and in another hot, grassy little hole southeast of Oberlin. They are common enough in these two places, which are quite unlike the haunts described by Kirtland and Jordan.

FAMILY XVIII. ATHERINIDÆ. THE SILVERSIDES.

61. Labidesthes sicculus Cope. BROOK SILVERSIDES.
[Jord. Man. 250. O. St. Surv. 111.]

A very slender rounded little fish: head long, pointed, flat above, transluscent green dotted with black: *sides with a broad silvery band, two dorsal fins.* Length 3½ inches.

Quite common in the lake, and in the large streams, below the dams.

FAMILY XIX. **CENTRARCHIDÆ.** THE SUNFISHES.

The members of this family are usually short and deep in the body, much compressed, scales large or moderate, closely adherent. dorsal fin continuous with 6 to 13 spines, anal with 3 to 8. All are carnivorous. (See plates 9, 10, 11.)

62. **Pomoxis sparoides** (Lacépède.) GRASS-BASS.

[Jord. Man. 298. O. St. Surv. 114.]

Body very much compressed, oblong, of a bright silvery olive color mottled with darker shadings, *6 anal and 7 dorsal spines.* Length 12 inches.

I have seen but two adults, both taken by Mr. Warden's pounds, near Lorain. Small ones of 2 or 3 inches are common enough, however, in the lower parts of Beaver Creek and Black River.

63. **Pomoxis annularis** Rafinesque. CRAPPIE.

[Jord. Man. 299. O. St. Surv. 113.]

This species is very similar to the preceding, from which it may be known by its having *six* spines in both dorsal and anal fins. Length 12 inches.

I have seen no adults, the young are common with the preceding species.

64. **Ambloplites rupestris** (Rafinesque.) ROCK-BASS.

[Jord. Man. 300. O. St. Surv. 124.]

Adult fish are quite plain-colored, somewhat striped longitudinally over a bronze-olive. The young are prettily mottled and blotched with black on a clear olive back ground. *10-12 dorsal spines, 5-7 anal.* Length 8 to 12 inches.

Common in the larger streams; sometimes taken by the pound-nets in the lake.

65. **Lepomis cyanellus** (Rafinesque). GREEN SUNFISH.

[Jord Man. 307. O. St. Surv. 122.]

Body oblong, mouth large, cheeks with blue stripes, opercular flap short with pale margins, *a conspicuous black spot at base of last rays of dorsal and anal fins, dorsal spines low, about equal to snout.* Length 5 to 7 inches.

Abundant in the upper part of small streams and in small ponds. I have not noticed it in the lake.

66. Lepomis pallidus (Mitchill). BLUE SUNFISH.

[Jord. Man. 313. O. St. Surv. 121.].

A plain-colored small-mouthed fish, young silvery, adults dusky *with a dark spot on last rays of anal and dorsal, dorsal spines high*, no blue on cheeks nor red on fins. Length about 10 inches. Not common. I have two large specimens taken in Mr. Warden's pound, and a few smaller ones seined in Black River.

67. Lepomis megalotis (Rafinesque). LONG-EARED SUNFISH.

[Jord. Man; 315. O. St. Surv. 118.]

A bright colored fish with neat, squarish looking scales, mouth small, *the ear flap long with pale margins in adult.* The young need to be carefully studied for identification. Attains a length of 6 inches. That it is extremely variable is shown by its list of 36 synonyms.

Rare. I took two specimens near the mouth of Black River, September 10, 1890, the only records.

68. Lepomis euryorus McKay.

[Jord. Man. 317.]

Body oblong, mouth large, dorsal spines medium, *scales on cheeks in 6 or 7 rows,* greenish, with some of the scales darker, giving a mottled appearance to the fish, opercular flap large (in adult) with a broad margin, tail and lower fins with orange margins.

I took seven specimens near Huron, July 6, 1891, and two near Lorain in September. At Huron they were associated with *L. cyanellus, L. gibbosus, Fundulus diaphanus,* and several species of *Notropis.*

The type specimen from Fort Gratiot, Lake Huron, was unique for several years, but in a recent letter Dr. Bean (U. S. F. C.) says: "We now have a fine, large example of *euryorus* from Minnesota in addition to the type." So far as I know this makes the third record.

69. Lepomis gibbosus (Linnæus). COMMON SUNFISH. "PUMPKIN-SEED."

[Jord. Man. 319. O. St. Surv. 116.]

Olive-green or bluish, the sides thickly spotted with orange, lower fins and chest of same color, *spines high, ear-flap black, tipped with bright scarlet.* Length 8 inches. (See plate 9.)

Very abundant below the riffles in the larger streams and in the bayous near the lake. A few are taken in the pounds. I have not found it above the dams, except in Camden lake, where they attain a large size.

The genus *Micropterus* is distinguished from other Centrarchidæ by the smaller scales and elongated body. (See plates 10 and 11.)

70. **Micropterus dolomieu** Lacépède. SMALL-MOUTHED BLACK-BASS.

[Jord. Man. 320. O. St. Surv. 125.]

Body elongated, rather stout, adult dark greenish, nearly uniform, young with golden green sides spotted and barred but no dark lateral band, *about 74 scales in lateral line*, mouth moderate sized, *scales on cheek in about 17 rows*. Length 1 to 2½ feet. (See plate 10.)

Common in the larger streams. Not so often seen among the lake fish as the next species.

71. **Micropterus salmoides** (Lacépède). LARGE-MOUTHED BLACK-BASS.

[Jord. Man. 321. O. St. Surv. 126.]

Like the preceding species but with a larger mouth and *68 or less scales in lateral line, scales on cheek in 10 rows*, dorsal fin deeply notched, the young have a dark lateral band. Length 1 to 2 feet. (See plate 11.)

More common in the lake than in the streams.

FAMILY XX. **PERCIDÆ.** THE PERCHES.

Rough-scaled fishes with two distinct dorsal fins, the first being spiny (6-15), *anal fin with 1 or 2 equal-sized spines*. (See plate 12.)

72. **Etheostoma pellucidum** Baird. SAND DARTER.

[Jord. Man. 322. O. St. Surv. 132.]

A very slender, *translucent, round* little fish, finely dotted above, a *series of square black blotches arranged in four rows down the back and sides*. Length 2½ inches.

Lake Erie and the larger streams. Not common.

73. **Etheostoma nigrum** Rafinesque. JOHNNY DARTER.

[Jord. Man. 326. O. St. Surv. 133.]

Yellowish grey, back speckled with brown, a *black bar from eye to snout*, sides with a series of small W-shaped blotches, *anal spine obscure*. Length 2½ inches.

Very common every where. One of the few species that may be depended upon when the seine is drawn.

74. **Etheostoma blennioides** Rafinesque. GREEN-SIDED DARTER.

[Jord. Man. 332. O. St. Surv. 135.]

Body stout and elongated, *head very blunt, mouth small and inferior*, color olive-green, spotted above, sides marked with about 8 Y-shaped bars. Length about 4 inches.

Vermillion River, scarce. I found them not uncommon in Sandusky Bay, where they were associated with Yellow Perch, Log Perch, and Sunfish.

75. **Etheostoma copelandi** (Jordan).

[Jord. Man. 333. O. St. Surv. 137.]

Body slender, head large and long, cheeks naked, opercles partly scaled, nape naked half way to first dorsal, ventral plates large; brownish-yellow with ten blotches on the sides. Dorsal XI-12, anal II-9, lateral line 4-53-8. Length 2⅓ inches.

Vermillion River, but one specimen taken.

76. **Etheostoma caprodes** Rafinesque. LOG-PERCH.

[Jord. Man. 337. O. St. Surv. 138.]

Body elongated, somewhat compressed, head long and pointed, color greenish-yellow *with about 15 zebra-like black bands*. Length 6 to 8 inches.

Not very common, though I have taken it in both of the rivers and in the lake. It was very abundant among the stonewort that carpets Sandusky Bay and Put-in-Bay, and it formed the bulk of the fishes that I saw among the terns' nests on Rattle Snake Island, July 13, 1891.

Most of the specimens have the nape of the neck naked (variety *zebra*, Agassiz), but the typical form, with the nape scaly, occurs in the proportion of about 1 in 3; some specimens show an intermediate stage. Many of my specimens show only 14 spines in the dorsal fin.

77. **Etheostoma peltatum** Stauffer. SHIELDED DARTER.

[Jord. Man. 339.]

Body rather stout, cheeks naked, olive green, with short black cross-bars on the back. Length 4 inches.

Rare. I have seen them only once, when two specimens were secured from Vermillion River.

78. **Etheostoma aspro** Cope & Jordan. BLACK-SIDED
DARTER.

[Jord. Man. 340. O. St. Surv. 142.]

Body elongated, rounded. greenish-yellow with dark markings
above, and about 7 dark oblong, sometimes partly confluent,
blotches on the sides. Length 3 to 4 inches. One of the prettiest
and hardiest of our darters.

Nowhere common, but found in most of the streams and in
the lake.

79. **Etheostoma wrighti** sp. nov.

On April 9, 1892, I took an *Etheostoma* in the Vermillion
River that presents several points of difference from those described.
It falls naturally into the group *Alvordius* Girard, and seems to be
related to *Etheostoma aspro*, from which it differs in having a
shorter spinous, and longer soft dorsal, larger scales, a stronger
spine on opercle, and smaller, more numerous blotches on the
sides.

The analysis is, dorsal X-14, anal II-11, lateral line 6-55-7,
premaxillaries not protractile, lateral line complete, ventral line
naked, mouth moderate, palatine teeth present, cheeks and opercles
scaly, nape naked except for a central line of embedded scales, color
(after being in alcohol over night) olivaceous, lighter beneath, sides
with eleven quadrate blotches, partly confluent, dark shadings on
back, fins plain, except the first dorsal, which has has two black
blotches, one on first spine midway up, the other longer, on last
three spines. Length 2⅝ inches; head 4 times in length, depth 5½.

Protracted rains have kept the river full of water, and prevented
farther collecting since this specimen was taken.

Believing it to be a new species, I propose the name of *wrighti*
in honor of Professor A. A. Wright.

80. **Etheostoma phoxocephalum** Nelson. LONG-
HEADED DARTER.

[Jord. Man. 341. O. St. Surv. 141.]

Body slender, rounded, mouth large, color yellowish-brown
with X-shaped lateral markings, more numerous than in *aspro*,
head very slender.

Rare. One specimen taken near Lorain.

81. **Etheostoma flabellare** Rafinesque.   FAN-TAILED
DARTER.
[Jord. Man. 354.   O. St. Surv. 149.]

A dusky, olive-colored little fish, each scale on upper half of
body bearing a black spot, which combined form a *series of about
eight longitudinal lines*, the males farther marked with dark cross-
bars, caudal fin broad with dark bars, *dorsal fin short and low*,
lower jaw distinctly projecting; in the males, the spines of the first
dorsal fin have fleshy tips.

Rare. I have seen but 3 specimens, all from the Vermillion
River near the water-works dam.

82. **Etheostoma cœruleum** Storer.   RAINBOW DARTER.
[Jord. Man. 361.   O. St. Surv. 152.]

Body rather short and thick, fins high, head large, olivaceous,
darker above, about 12 bars of indigo running obliquely backward
with orange between, brighter in the males than in the females.
Length 2½ inches.

One of the most common darters, usually found in swift-run-
ning parts of the larger streams.

83. **Perca flavescens** (Mitchill).   YELLOW PERCH.
[Jord Man. 369.   O. St. Surv. 129.]

There is little need of describing this well known fish. The
rich yellow color and six broad dusky bands, short thick body and
head are familiar.   There is a good deal of variation in color,
some specimens from the lake being pale green without bands,
while those caught from among weeds are apt to be darker and
more spotted, but it is never silvery like the white bass, and the
deep body separates it from all other perches.   Length about 15
inches.   (See plate 12.)

Common in the lake and lower portions of the rivers, not detected above the dams.

84. **Stizostedion vitreum** (Mitchill).   BLUE-PIKE.
[Jord. Man. 370.   O. St. Surv. 131.]

Body quite elongated, head long, with wide mouth, first dorsal
fin high, nearly plain *except a large black blotch on base of the last
two or three spines; second dorsal with 21 rays*, bluish or yellowish
grey, mottled with brassy above.   Reaches a length of three feet,
and a weight of 20 (to 40?) pounds.

Very common in the lake, entering the streams occasionally. This is one of the most valuable food-fishes taken in the pounds.

85. **Stizostedion canadense** (C. H. Smith). SAUGER.
[Jord. Man. 371. O. St. Surv. 130.]

Body shaped like the preceding but not so much arched in the back, *dorsal fins with two or three rows of dark spots, second dorsal with 17 or 18 rays*. color olive or greyish with dark mottlings which form about three bands in young specimens. Length 18 inches, weight not often more than 2½ pounds.

Common in the lake, entering the streams oftener than the last species.

FAMILY XXI. **SERRANIDÆ.** THE SEA-BASS.

86. **Roccus chrysops** (Rafinesque). WHITE BASS.
[Jord. Man. 373. O. St. Surv. 127.]

A perch-like fish, but with *three* spines in anal fin, *silvery white with five or six dark longitudinal lines*. Length 10 to 15 inches. (See plate 13.)

Quite common in the lake. ascending the streams to the dams. Mr. George Dewey reports that it occurs near Kipton, far above the dams. This one representative of a large salt-water family is supposed by some to be the land-locked form of the Striped Bass (*Roccus lineatus*).

FAMILY XXII. **SCIÆNIDÆ.** THE DRUMFISHES.

87. **Aplodinotus grunniens** (Rafinesque). SHEEPS-HEAD. LAKE DRUM.
[Jord. Man. 398. O. St. Surv. 156.]

Body oblong, with symmetrically arched back, soft dorsal much longer than the spiny part. color clear silvery white in young, often smoky brown in larger specimens, *the second anal spine several times larger and stouter than the first.* (See plate 14.)

A worthless fish, very common in the lake. I have seen large specimens on the riffles of the Vermillion among the suckers in April, and young ones are common just below the dam in Black River in August and September. The otolithic ear-bones of this species are the "lucky stones" that are often found on the lake beach.

FAMILY XXIII. COTTIDÆ. THE SCULPINS.

88. Cottus richardsoni Agassiz. STAR-GAZER. "MUD HEAD."

[Jord. Man. 406. O. St. Surv. 161.]

A big-headed little fish with a tapering body, *large pectoral fins*, short, low spinous dorsal fin, longer, higher soft dorsal, eyes set close together on top of head: color reddish, blotched and speckled with darker. Length 3 to 6 inches.

Common in Spring Brook and Chance Creek, not detected elsewhere in the county.

FAMILY XXIV. GADIDÆ. THE CODFISHES.

89. Lota maculosa (Le Sueur). BURBOT. LAWYER.

[Jord. Man. 453. O. St. Surv. 163.]

A long, large-mouthed, small-scaled fish that looks like a cross between a catfish and an eel, brownish-yellow, usually thickly mottled with darker, belly lighter, *lower jaw with one long barbel*. (See plate 4.)

Common in the lake, not detected in the streams.

LIST OF THE PLATES.

			Page.
Plate	1.	Lepidosteus platystomus. Short-nosed Garpike.	10
		Dorosoma cepedianum. Gizzard-shad.	21
Plate	2.	Amia calva. Bowfin.	11
		Anguilla rostrata. Eel.	25
Plate	3.	Semotilus atromaculatus. Chub.	20
		Moxostoma macrolepidotum. Mullet.	15
Plate	4.	Lota maculosa. Burbot.	33
		Hiodon tergisus. Mooneye.	21
Plate	5.	Acipenser rubicundus. Sturgeon.	10
Plate	6.	Ameiurus melas. Bullhead.	12
Plate	7.	Coregonus artedi. Lake-herring.	22
Plate	8.	Esox masquinongy. Maskalonge.	24
Plate	9.	Lepomis gibbosus. Sunfish.	27
Plate	10.	Micropterus dolomieu. Small-mouthed Black-bass.	28
Plate	11.	Micropterus salmoides. Large-mouthed Black-bass.	28
Plate	12.	Perca flavescens. Yellow Perch.	31
Plate	13.	Roccus chrysops. White-bass.	32
Plate	14.	Aplodinotus grunniens. Sheepshead.	32

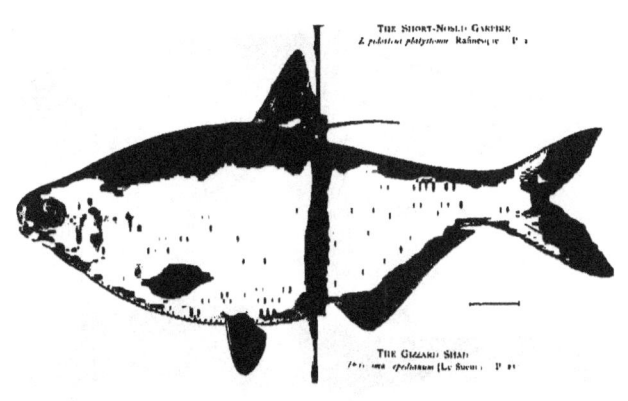

THE SHORT-NOSED GARPIKE
L. platostomus Rafinesque P. 1

THE GIZZARD SHAD
Dorosoma cepedianum (Le Sueur) P. 41

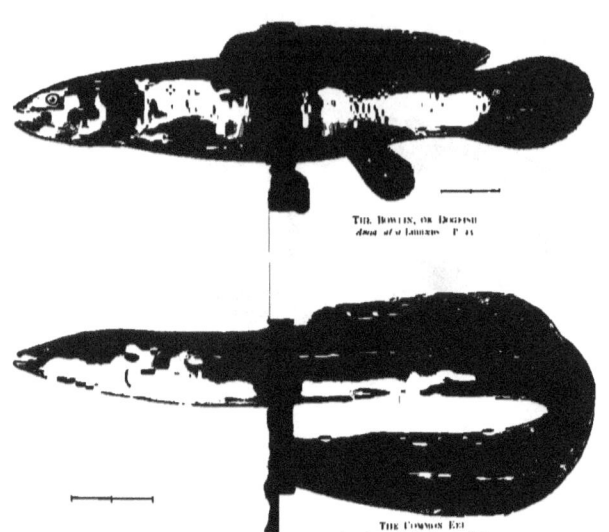

THE BOWFIN, OR DOGFISH
Amia alva Linnaeus P. 41

THE COMMON EEL
Anguilla rostrata La Sueur P. 43

PLATE 4

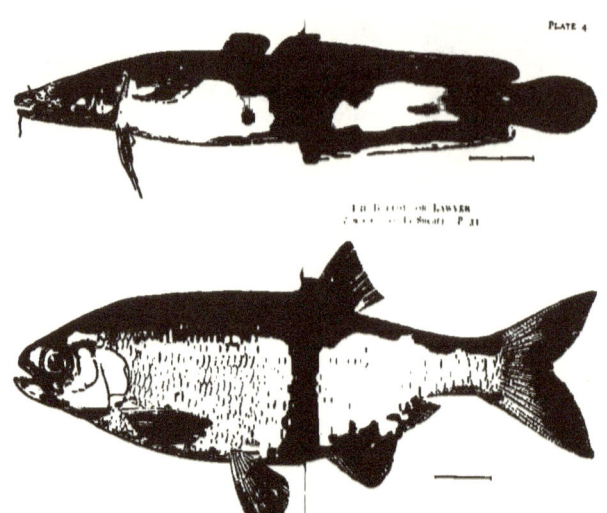

Fig. 1. EEL-POUT OR LAWYER
Fig. 2. LAKE SMELT P. 31

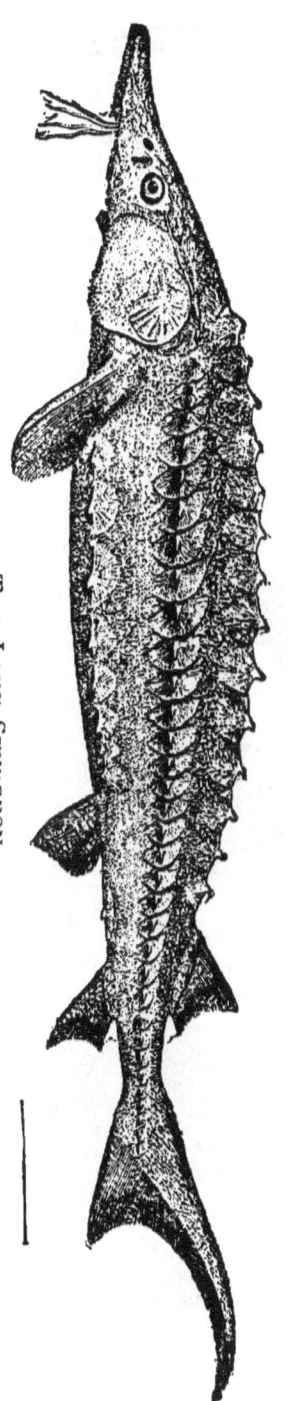

THE LAKE STURGEON.

Acipenser rubicundus Le Sueur. P. 10.

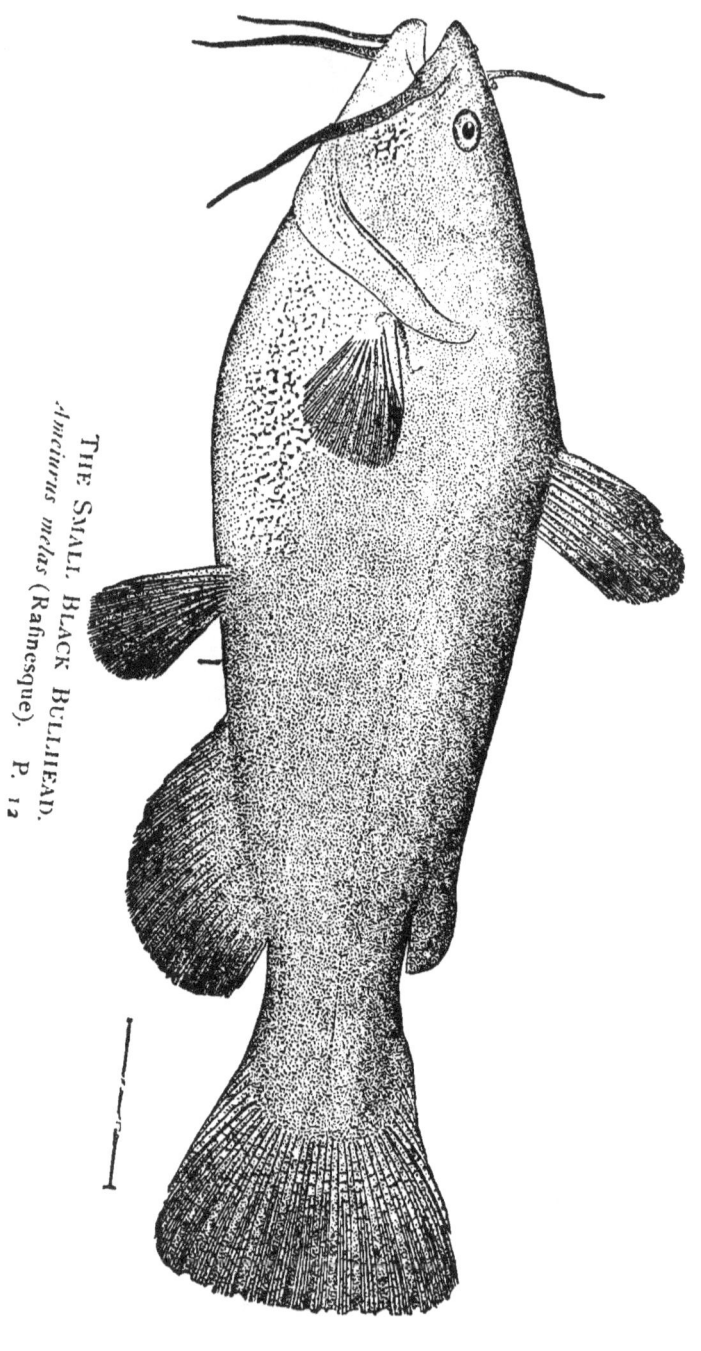

THE SMALL BLACK BULLHEAD.
Amiurus melas (Rafinesque). P. 12

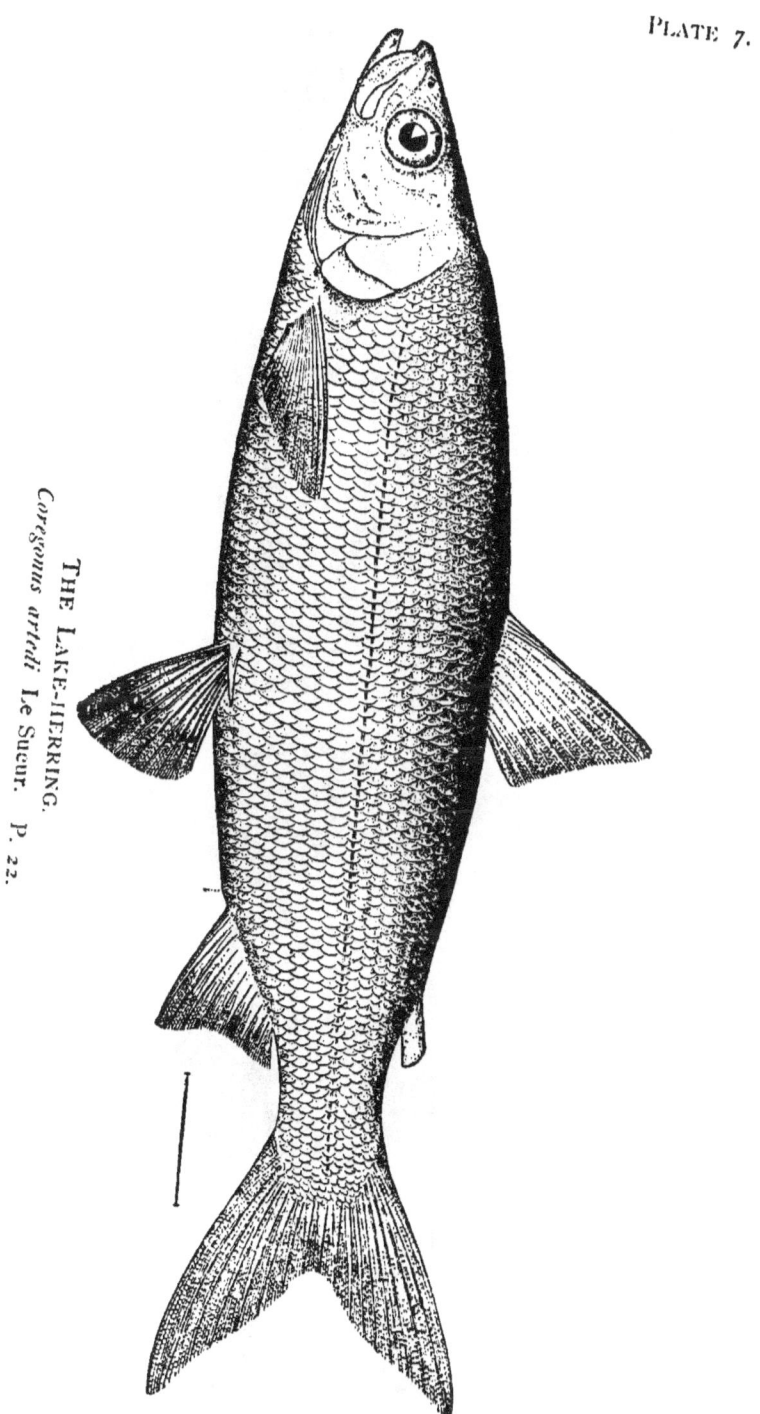

PLATE 7.

THE LAKE-HERRING.
Coregonus artedi Le Sueur. P. 22.

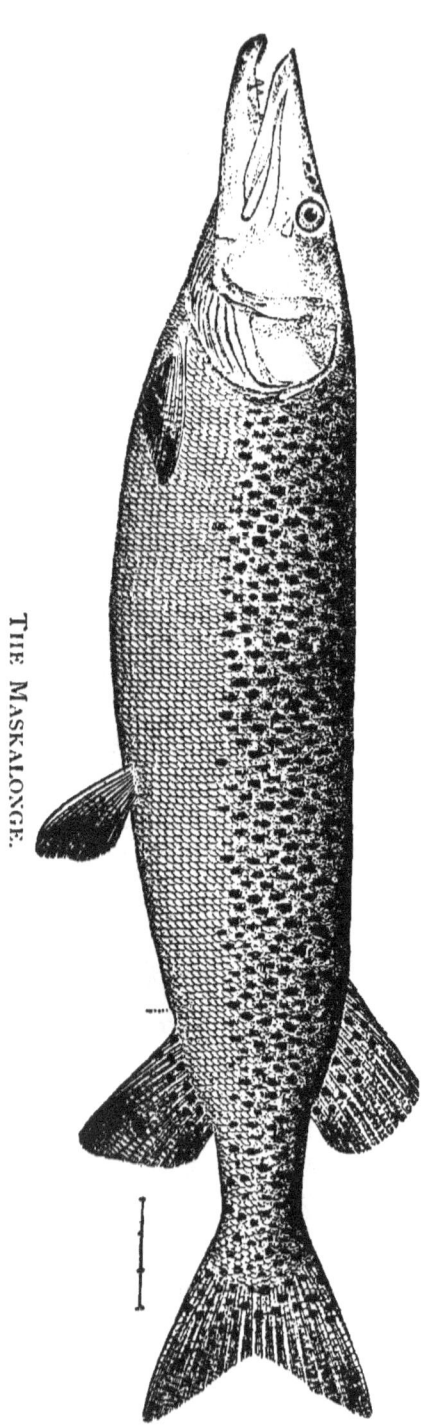

THE MASKALONGE.

Esox masquinongy (Mitchill). P. 24.

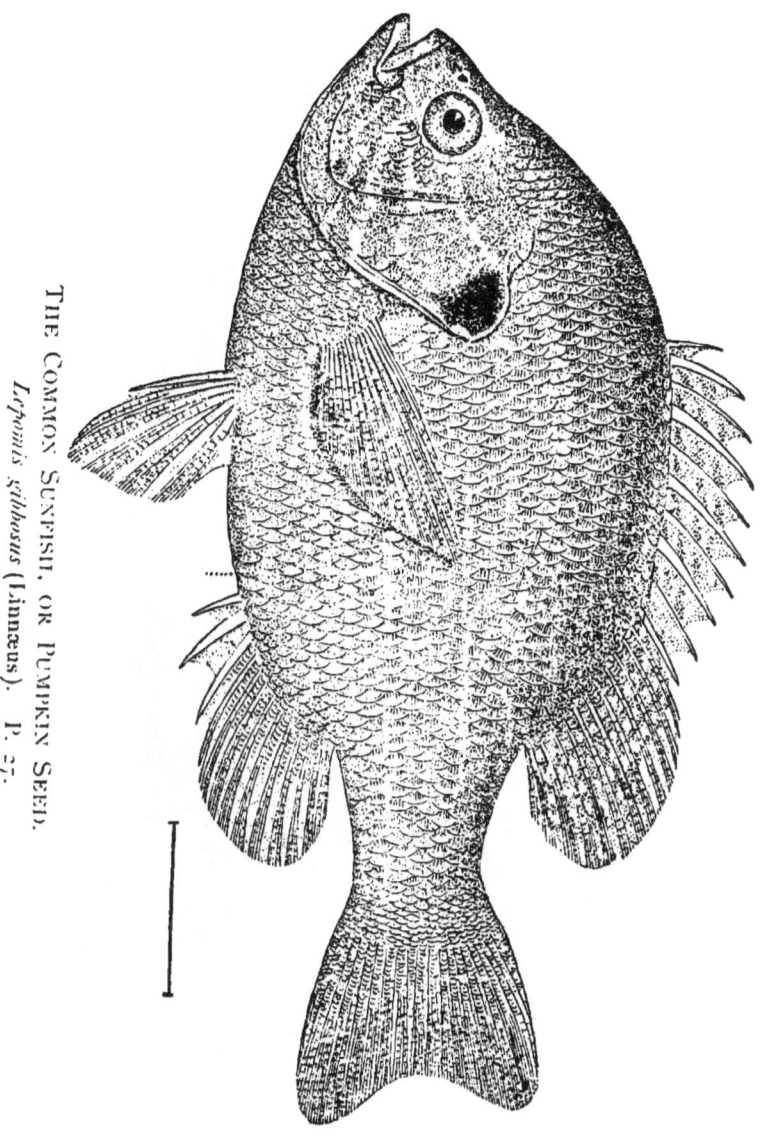

THE COMMON SUNFISH, OR PUMPKIN SEED.
Lepomis gibbosus (Linnæus). P. 47.

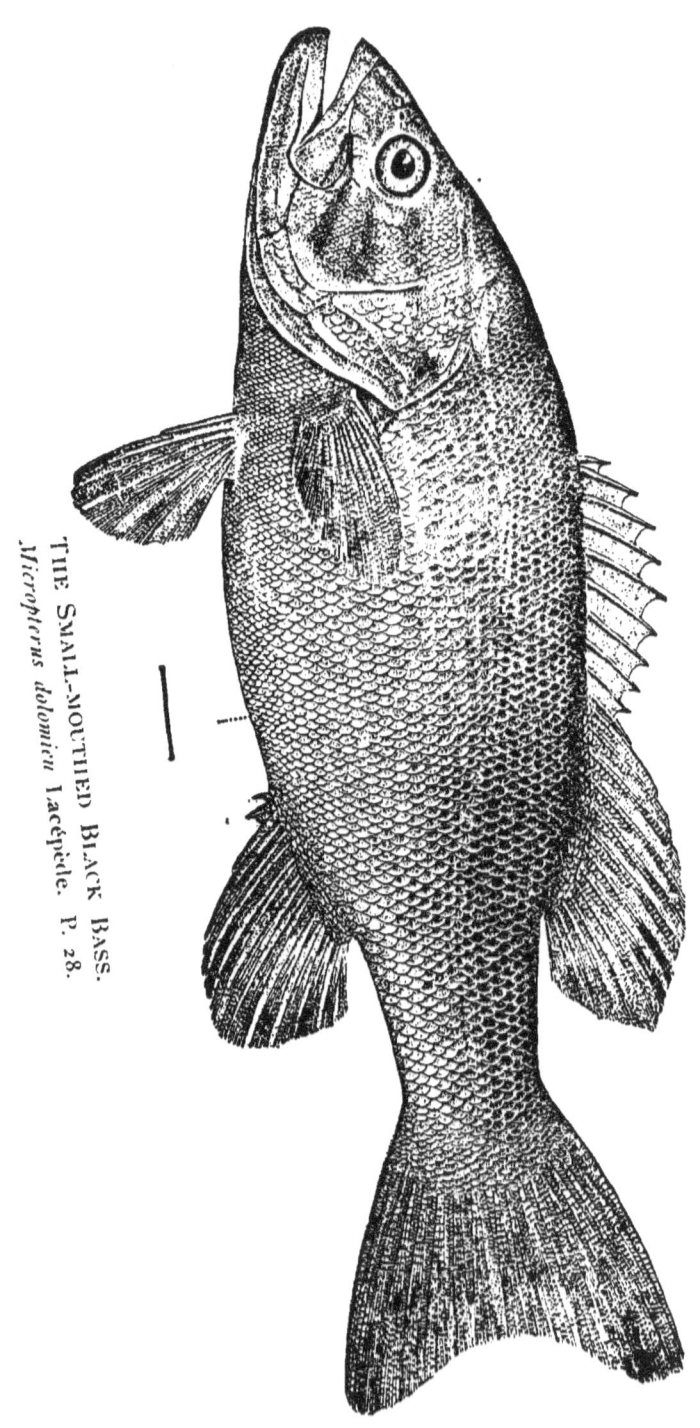

THE SMALL-MOUTHED BLACK BASS.
Micropterus dolomieu Lacépède. P. 28.

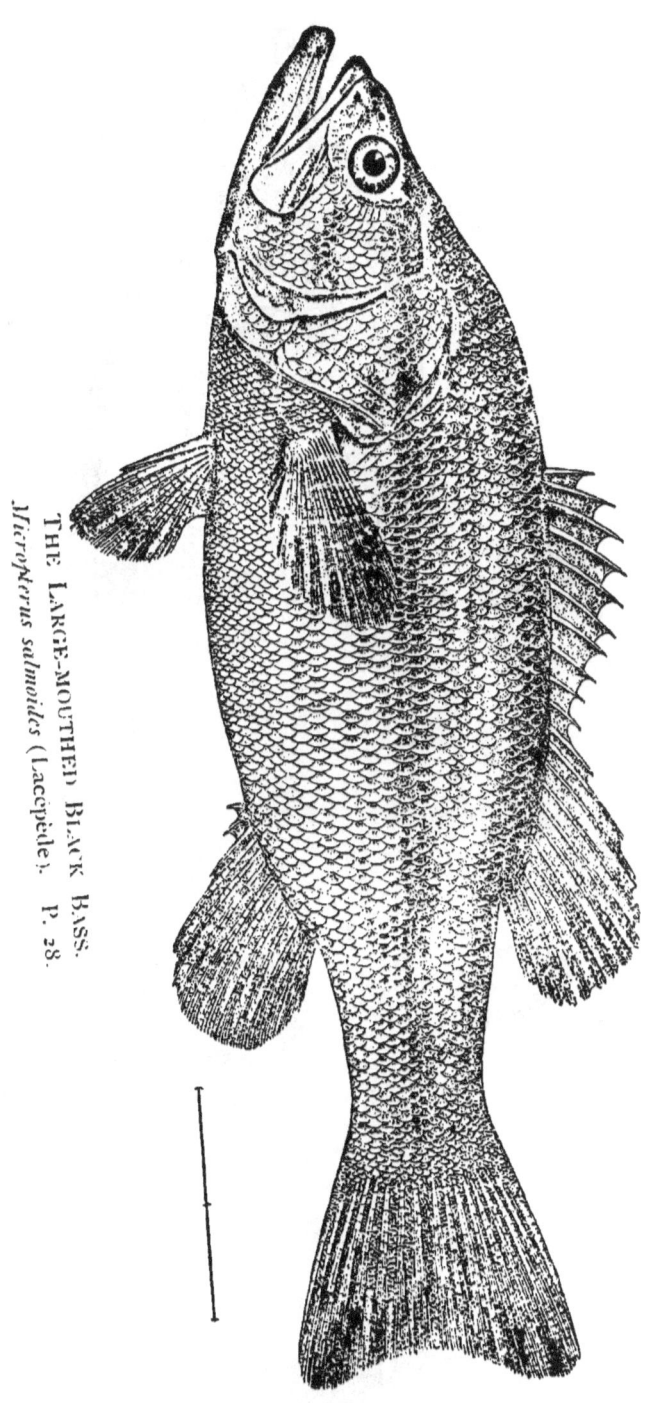

THE LARGE-MOUTHED BLACK BASS.
Micropterus salmoides (Lacepède). P. 28.

PLATE 12.

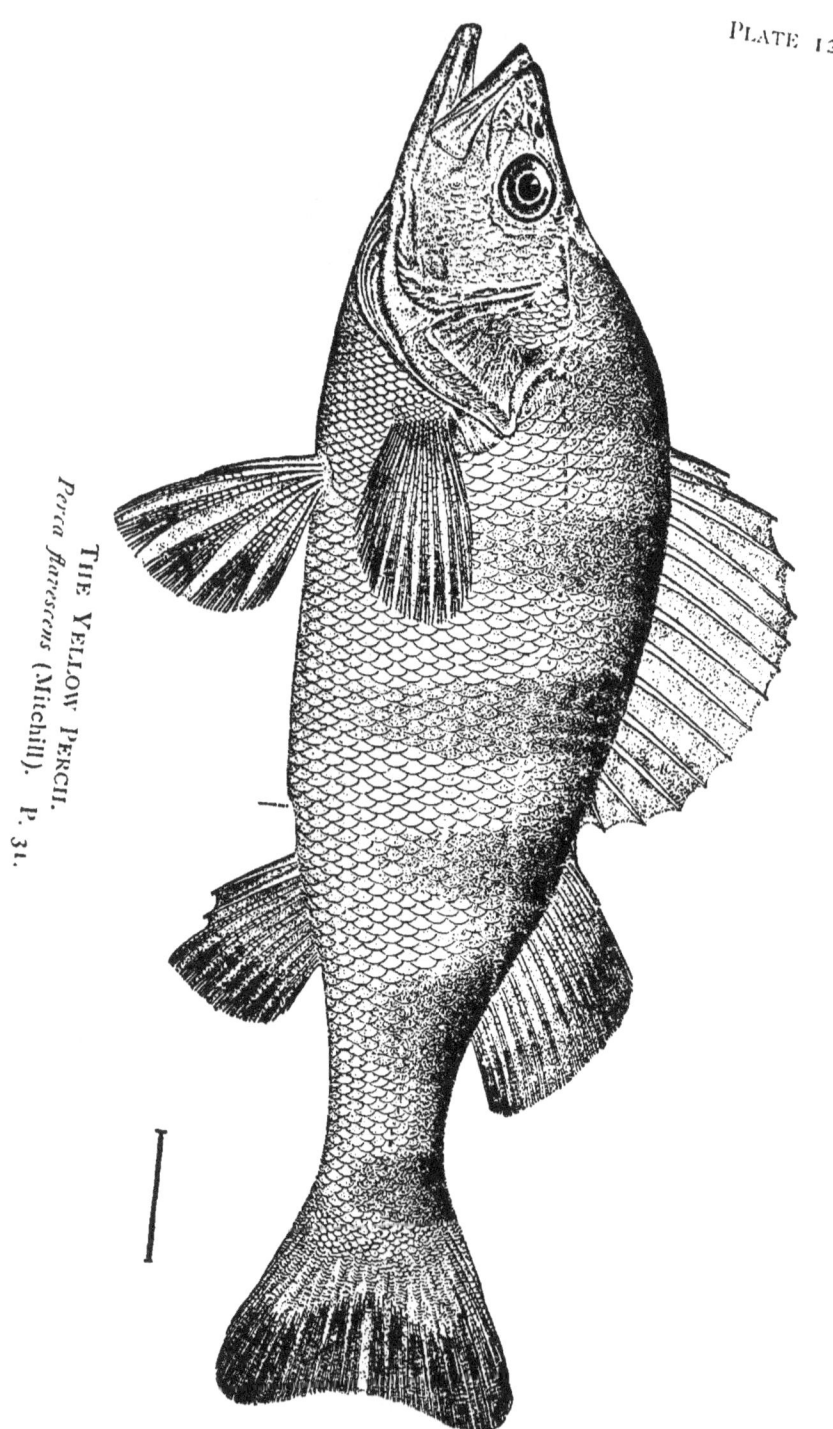

THE YELLOW PERCH.
Perca flavescens (Mitchill). P. 34.

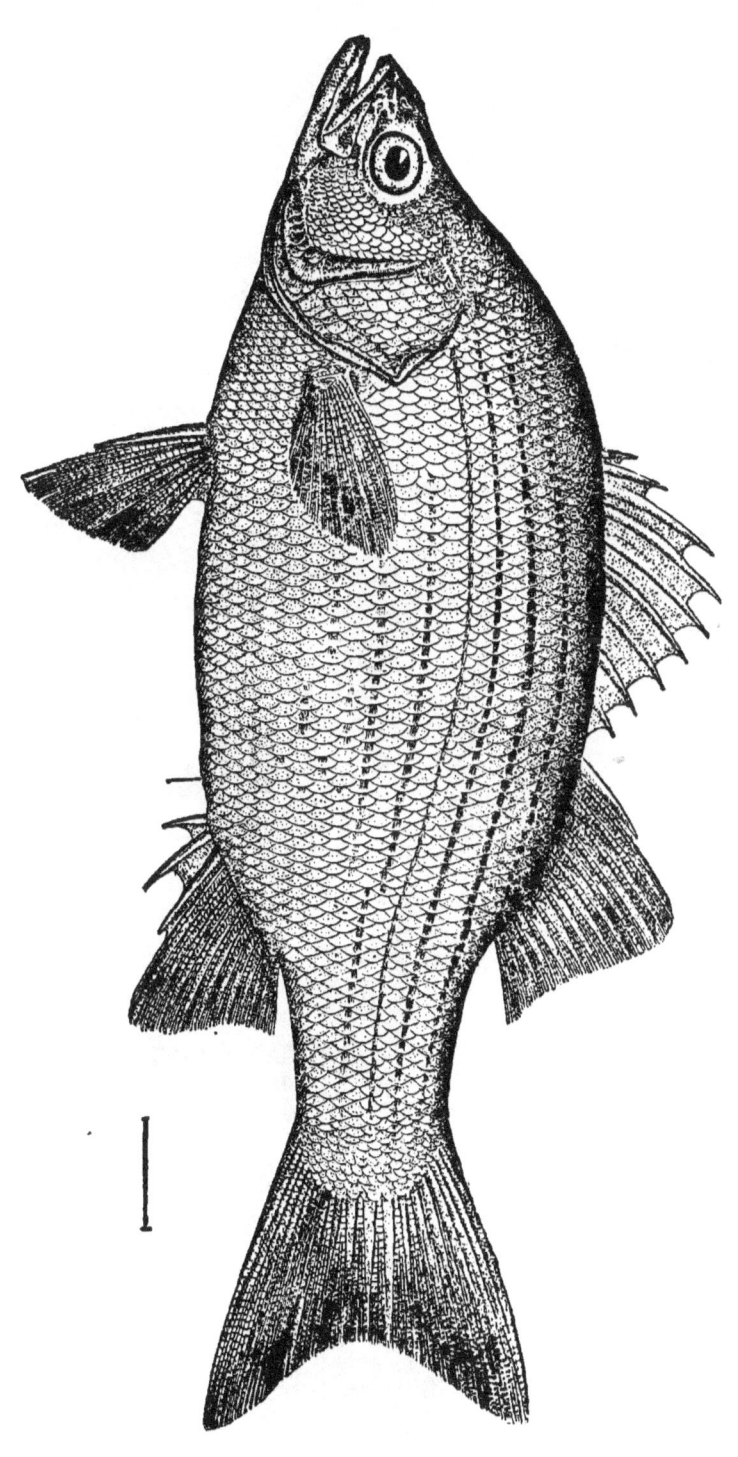

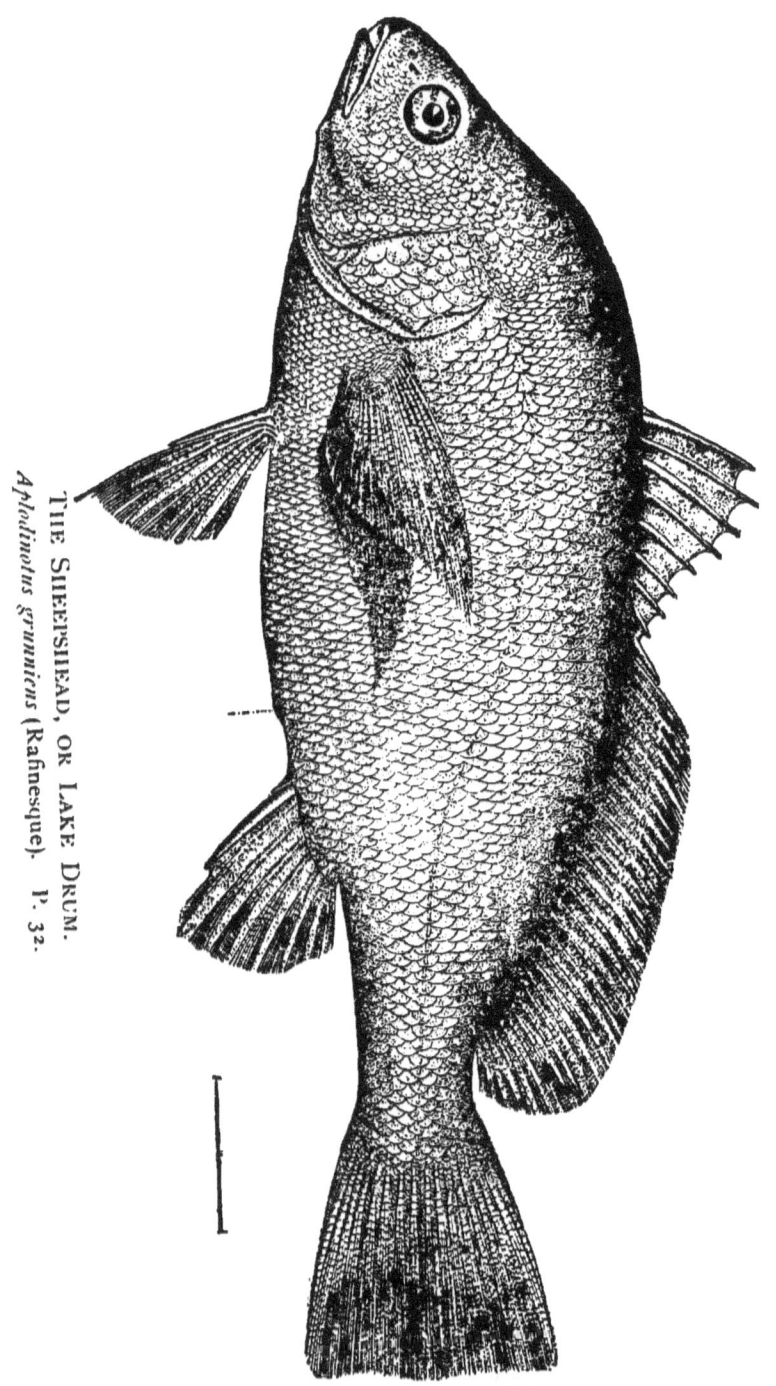

THE SHEEPSHEAD, OR LAKE DRUM.
Aplodinotus grunniens (Rafinesque). P. 32.

www.ingramcontent.com/pod-product-compliance
Lightning Source LLC
Chambersburg PA
CBHW021236260626
47172CB00002B/796